A Cat On Mars

A Rescued Tail

All rights reserved

Copyright © 2017

By A Nation

Published 2018

ISBN-978-1979183857

ACKNOWLEDGEMENTS

I want to thank those that gave me support and tolerated my persistence in writing my story; they are by first names only as they know who they are: Yuma Writer's on the Edge club, Meleesa, and Shirley.

Copyright

No part of this book may be reproduced or transmitted in any form or by any means, electronic or mechanical, including photocopying, recording, or by any information storage and retrieval system without permission in writing from the publisher.

This is a work of fiction. Names, characters, businesses, places, events and incidents are either the products of the author's imagination or used in a fictitious manner. Any resemblance to actual persons, living or dead, or actual events is purely coincidental.

A. Nation

<u>Domino Sagas 2422 – 2424 A.D.:</u>
    Similar But Not the Same   – Saga 1
    Found - The Lost Ones   - Saga 4
    Return - There's No Easy Way – Saga 5

    CrossRoads   A Moment of Decision – Saga 3

<u>Blackhawk Files – 2407-2432 A.D.</u>
    Best Friends – Prequel Outtake
    Deflection   A Race Against Time   - Saga 2
    Desert Shock - Secrets Never Stay Hidden   - Saga 6
    Fatal Error – Death by Innocence   - Saga 7
    The Takers – In the Dark of Night   - Saga 8
    High Flyer – Life and Times of Charlie Dane

Sequel
<u>Quest Series</u>
    Eye of the Matrix – The Stone Map   Quest 1
    Eye of the Throne –Destiny   Quest 2

<u>Urban Series:</u>
    Hobnobby's Story - Prequel
    Where Did They Go? -– Urban Fantasy 1
    The Pottery Sale -   Urban Fantasy 2
    The Cruise – Lost At Sea   Urban Fantasy 3
    A Witch Comes A Haunting - Urban Fantasy 4

<u>Travel Series:</u>
    The Lost Jewel - Prequel
    Mystery Along the Danube –   - Travel 1
    Mystery Along the Italian Coast – Travel 2

<u>Visit A. Nation's Amazon page:</u>
    http://www.amazon.com/A-Nation/e/B00SUHXM6E
    to see what books are currently on sale.

A. Nation

Table of Contents

Saved
Rescued
New Home
Moving On
Mars
Keeping Warm
Weeks Later
Earth
The Farm
Commotion
Red Planet

A. Nation

This a compilation of the Frederick's adventure on Mars and Earth.

Saved

Mary Ann McCarthy rummaged about in the alley dumpster for thrown away wrapped bread, recycles or another article of clothing she could wear or sell during the cooler months to come. She was homeless but didn't think she was. She had places she could stay the nights with others in the same predicament as she.

She heard a squeak but brushed the sound off to the creaking of the dumpster as she pushed a cardboard box out of her way. Mary had to hurry. The Montrose garbage truck would be coming down the alley in an hour. Then she heard a faint cry like a baby but much higher pitched against the background noise of the air cars on the street.

"Oh Gawd, I hope someone didn't throw a baby in here," she muttered pulling newspapers away from where she heard the sound.

The tiny cry squealed again. As she lifted up more trash paper there were two dark eyes staring back at her.

"Well, what's this?" she asked, looking down at the frightened fuzzy handful.

"Oh, you poor thing. Someone just threw you away like garbage."

A. Nation

With one hand, she scooped up the tiny black and white body.

"Oh, you may not make it," she frowned as she felt the kitten's rib bones under the thin skin.

Placing the scrawny animal into her sweater pocket, she began pushing her wire cart down the alley toward the busy street.

"I'll find you a safe place. I can't take care of you and myself."

Glancing in both directions down the sidewalk, Mary Ann remembered a veterinary office not far away.

Mary, now in her seventies, couldn't pay the mounting bills of keeping up a home after her husband died a few years ago. Taking to the streets was scary at first among thugs strong enough to do honest work who instead tried to steal what little money she carried. Soon she met many more like herself in the safer areas of town. On occasion, she would go to one of the shelters during bad weather for just a good meal to eat and a shower but would leave after a few days.

After trudging for three blocks pulling her loaded basket of found treasures, Mary Ann arrived at the pet hospital. She had seen those people who had the means to take their animals into the Downtown Pet Clinic. "Surely," she thought, "they would take care of this little piece of fluff."

She looked in her knitted pocket of the old sweater she had worn for years to make sure the kitten was still alive.

A. Nation

Two black eyes stared back at her. That was all she needed to walk in through the metal door.

As soon as she entered the sanitary reception office, the girl adorned with an upswept hair style behind the desk, jumped up.

"You can't come in here. This is not a hospital for humans," she said hurrying around the counter. Many times some of the homeless people would want the veterinary doctor to help them with a cut or a broken arm because the cost was lower than at the hospital.

"I ain't here for myself, sweety. Here, I found this little guy. I can't keep him. Is there anything you can do for him?" Mary Ann asked, placing the scrawny kitten on the counter.

"Oh my, oh, let me get the doctor," the receptionist said, changing her tune as she returned to her desk. She wrapped the black kitten into a terry cloth towel she withdrew from under the counter.

The woman whisked the orphan into the back room, leaving Mary Ann to wait. After a few more minutes, she decided she wanted to leave, when the young woman reappeared without the kitten.

"The doctor will have to treat him for infection and mites. We will have to keep him overnight. If you had him in your sweater, you should get it washed as soon as you can. You can pick him up in a couple of days."

"Lady, I can't keep the thing. I just couldn't see him staying in that dumpster. You keep him. Maybe when he fills out some, somebody will want to take care of him. Sorry, I have to go."

"But–."

Mary Ann walked out of the door, pulling her heavy cart behind her. The young lady stared. She wasn't going to run after the old woman. She knew many like her couldn't afford to care and feed a pet.

After a few days had passed, the black and white male cat began to heal and gained strength under the care of the veterinary. The receptionist couldn't take it home. She owned two cats, the maximum allowed in her apartment. The veterinary hospital had a policy if an abandoned cat or dog stays two weeks, the veterinary must take them to the animal shelter. There the employees knew that the animal will have a higher percentage of being put to sleep.

"What do we call him?" she asked the doctor.

"You choose. If we can get him adopted, the new owners may want to change the name. Let the pet store over on Fortieth Street know that we have this little guy. Maybe someone who is looking for a young cat will want him."

"Okay," she said, petting the kitten and placing him into one of the cages for hospitalized animals.

The black kitten stared back at her. He was still too weak to protest his enclosure but the warm soft towel was the best he had since leaving his mother. He curled up and went fast to sleep.

The next day, the doctor's nurse gave him some nasty tasting medicine, a thorough bath, and cleaned his cage. She placed a new white towel down and set him in the middle before latching the wire frame.

The kitten sat up and looked next door and noticed a small animal something like himself sleeping in the other cage.

"Mew"

"Huh?" the hairy critter said, picking up its head to look around.

The kitten steadied his legs and walked over to the dividing grill between their cages.

"Mew!" he said louder.

"Cat? Oh, I'm too sick to bother with you. Go away."

"What's wrong with you?"

"I don't know. But my rear hurts."

"I miss my mom," replied the kitten.

"You're alone here?" the dog asked, perking up his ears.

"I guess."

The dog struggled to stand and flopped down near the cage edge closest to the kitten's side.

"Uhh, I feel tired. Go to sleep cat."

The black and white kitten sniffed the animal. An antiseptic smell permeated from the dog's body. Wrinkling his nose, he curled up next to the wire divider where the dog's fur stuck through and fell asleep.

A. Nation

Rescued

A week and a half had passed and the kitten became stronger and more filled out. When cat customers had entered the veterinary, the receptionist would always ask if they would like a handsome male kitten that had been fixed. Most would either say they had too many cats, or they weren't interested. With great sadness, the receptionist called the local animal shelter to pick up the black and white kitten.

She set the cat in a carrier by the door and left the office. She didn't want to be there when the shelter people came to take the kitten away. Returning from lunch, she noticed the carrier with the kitten was gone.

Later that afternoon, a young blond haired woman walked in, looked around and came forward to the front desk.

"Yes, may I help you?" the receptionist asked.

"Maybe, I was just over at the pet store on Fortieth and they said you might have a cat I could be interested in. I was hoping they had one I liked but they didn't," the young lady said.

"Oh, I'm sorry, but the kitten was just picked up by the shelter," she said. But if you hurry, they close in an hour."

"Which shelter?"

"The one on Boone Road–outside of town.

"Thanks," Alice said and ran out to her rented air car.

Racing through the busy traffic across town, she listened to her car's GPS to find the small animal shelter. The time was now 4:45pm.

Five minutes to the hour, she parked the car in front of the older building. She hopped out and turned the handle on the front door of the small building. It was locked.

"No, you got five minutes. Let me in," she wailed, knocking on the wooden door.

Then she heard the door unlock.

"Yes? We're almost closed," said an older woman wearing a flowered dress.

"A cat was recently brought over here from the veterinary. Can I look at it?" she said out of breath.

The woman smiled and opened the door further.

"Over here, we were just about to put him in the back."

Alice bent down to the floor and picked up the carrier. Looking inside she could see two tiny black eyes staring back at her. She opened the carrier and scooped the soft kitten out.

"I'll take him. What do you need from me?"

"We were told his medical bills came to $110. We have a deal with the vet. If you pay half, our grant pays the rest.

"I'll pay all of it."

"First I need to have you fill out this form on your background. Do you work during the day?"

"I do, but I plan to take this little feller with me to work. Does he need anything special to eat? Any allergies?" she asked as she began filling out the form with her name and address.

"Nothing about that was written on his bio, uh, Miss Alice Morgan," the lady said, reading where Alice had written her name.

"Have you ever owned a cat?" the lady asked.

"Long, long time ago when I was a child. I had an all-black cat back then," she said filling out the required lines.

Alice handed the form back and paid the expenses.

The lady gave Alice a copy of the form.

"Please give him a good home," she said to Alice.

"I will. Thank you so much," Alice said looking in the carrier opening at the two black eyes peering back up at her.

"Mew" said the kitten.

"Does he have a name?" she asked the woman.

The older lady just shook her head.

"Okay, thanks," Alice said walking outside toward her car.

The front door behind her closed and the latch locked.

Alice turned and walked out of the animal shelter wondering what to call her new friend.

Hopping into her rented air car, she placed the carrier next to her and snapped the seat belt around it. The year was 2422 and she was about to enter the space program. She had studied more about the vocation after her divorce

A. Nation

and campaigned for animal studies to be taken in space. When she was accepted, they said yes but only for a cat. Now that she had found one, she'll have to train the kitten on behavior. Chuckling to herself about the release form at the veterinary, she wondered what the receptionist would do if she told her that the cat was going to the Moon.

Talking to the kitten on the way back to her apartment, "I had a funny uncle that loved to get dressed up in a tuxedo for dinner even if it wasn't a formal affair. His name was Frederick. That's what I'll call you, Frederick."

"Mew," said the kitten who heard only 'blah, blah, Frederick.'

A. Nation

New Home

"Oh, darn, it's beginning to rain. We're almost there, Frederick," Alice said, gearing the wheels down onto the wet pavement.

The vibration from under the carrier was like nothing this young kitten had ever experienced before. Looking out through the carrier's screen door, Frederick could see a blond haired human. He bent his neck looking around and found they were both in a larger carrier. He tried to protest the long ride but the human beside him kept talking in a soothing voice.

"I will have to train you on leg weights, but you'll get used to them. This will be so exciting when we go to the Moon."

He didn't understand what she said but the excitement in her voice sounded happy.

The car came to a sudden stop. After the woman fussed around to add to her shoulders what he thought were additional skins, he felt himself and the carrier lifted out of the vehicle. The human ran through the falling rain causing his body to bump from side to side against the canvas container. His whiskers twitched at the humidity in the air.

A. Nation

"Meow," he bellowed when a few drops of rain splashed against his face through the mesh fabric.

"Almost home, Frederick," he heard the woman say as she ran up the apartment steps into a warmer and dryer location.

Alice pressed the elevator button and stepped into the compartment. Another woman stepped in after her.

"What do you have there?" she said bending down to look in the carrier. "A kitten. Is that okay with the manager?"

"Yes, I already asked him. We won't be staying long, I have a job coming up and Frederick, here, will be going with me."

The elevator came to a stop.

"That's nice. Good day," the lady said and walked out into the hallway.

A few floors higher, the elevator came to a stop again and Alice stepped out. Her apartment was two doors down. She set the carrier down near the door to locate her room key in one of her pant pockets.

"Ah, here we are," she said, swiping the card through the slot.

Once again, Frederick felt himself rising into the air and carried to a corner of the room.

"Well, here's your water and some food. Now, you be nice so I can let you out," she said, unzipping the door flap.

A. Nation

She knew from experience some animals, that were unfamiliar with their surroundings, will lash out first until they feel safe. At first she noticed the kitten seemed unsure about what to do so she backed away to give the animal some space.

"Take your time. I'm going to get out of these wet clothes," she said as she stripped off her wet jacket to hang it over a chair back. All he heard was 'blah, blah, blah,' as she walked into another room.

His eyes followed the woman who took off her shoes and placed them near a square slot in the floor near the far wall. She then filled up a water bowl and opened a can of cat food. After scraping the meal into another bowl, she left the room.

He poked one white paw out of the carrier and then another. He sniffed the water bowl and began drinking, and then he smelled the food nearby. The wet food smelled and tasted good since he hadn't eaten for a long time.

After filling his small tummy, he trotted over to the human's shoes, drying near the floor slot. Warm air was rushing from the opening. He jumped back and edged closer to figure out how this could work. He turned when the human walked back into the room and left again. He wanted to see where she was going.

This other room was as large as the first one but in the center was a raised platform with cloth draped over the top and down the sides. Giving the billowy material a pat on one corner, he extended his claws without realizing it, and began to climb the mountain before him.

"Oh, no you don't," he heard the woman say who grabbed him around his middle.

"Maybe when you're litter trained. In fact, let's do that now."

She carried him over to a tray filled with clumpy material. After twenty minutes of making him stay and pressing his rear down, she left him alone for a few minutes.

"No sense wearing you out," she said, walking away and disappeared back into the other room.

By the third day of his new found environment, he was litter trained and knew when he would be fed. His human stayed in what she called a bedroom most of the day tapping on something above his head. He had to see what that was.

While she left the room, he found leverage on an open drawer to climb on and from there he managed to jump up to the top of this table formation. On the surface he spotted a flat board with raised bumps. His whiskers could sense heat being emitted as he positioned his body over the object.

"Oh, Frederick. I can't get anything done with you in the way," the woman said, picking up the kitten and placing him back on the floor.

"Meow," he balked.

"Eat as much as you can, for tomorrow we travel," she said, returning to her tapping. "Oh, I almost forgot. Frederick I need you to get used to these weights on your paws."

He watched her stand up to pull out another drawer high over his head. She took out some wraps and began winding them around his legs above the paws.

"They aren't real heavy now, but in time as you grow I'll add a little more to them," she said.

Frederick didn't like them as he jiggled a paw every time he took a step. He struggled over to his bedding in the main room and lay down while he tried his best to lick them off. The fabric was soft but tasteless.

After a day he gave up on the odd attire. The human said something and vanished behind the door. Every few minutes, he would wander around looking for her. A few hours passed, and the door opened. The woman had returned with large bags and a box.

"Look what I got you, a litter contained kennel. You're getting too big for that little carrier. What do you think?" she said sliding the new container toward him.

He peered into the plastic kennel and backed out. He wanted to see what was in the box. The human left the room and he looked in the mysterious container and jumped in. He felt all the edges and the dark recesses in the corners.

The woman returned from the bedroom.

A. Nation

"I just remembered, we have to make sure I have your permits and vaccination papers handy," she said, reaching into the depths of her large purse to make sure they were secure inside.

That night, he could feel the humidity rise in the apartment as the human was boiling water on the stove. He watched her as she dipped out long white strands onto a plate. She poured another dish of red sauce over the mound of food. He licked both sides of his nose to taste the aroma in the air.

The woman placed her meal down on the table and left of locate a can of parmesan cheese in one of the high cupboards. He took this opportunity to spring up into the tall chair. His short legs didn't have enough push but he hooked his claws into the cushion and pulled himself up to the edge of the table. Sniffing the pile of sauce, he jumped into the plate.

"Feddy!" the human yelled, dropping the can of cheese.

Frederick had red sauce flowing down his head and paws. Scared as to what the woman was yelling about, he ran off the table and across the floor until she grabbed him by the scuff of his neck.

"Oh, you naughty boy, now we'll have to wash you."

She carried him at arm's length over a hard depression in the counter.

A. Nation

He had been in rain before but all this water in the was downright wet and warm. He received a good scrubbing but the human wouldn't let him get away. At last, she wrapped him into a towel and brought him back near the table.

"First I'm going to heat up what's left of my dinner and get you dried out," she said.

"Yeow," he protested.

The heating box made a ding sound and she put him back on the floor. He shook and shook until he made his way over to the heat vent.

He shivered for a short time as he tried to find comfort in his bed. Frederick looked up at the woman and noticed she finished eating her food. She stood up and stroked his fur to see how dry he was.

"Much better. I'll get you some food of your own," she said.

The next morning, Alice hurried back and forth while she cleaned the apartment for the next renter. Her cat followed her wherever she stopped. She filled the bathtub with a small amount of water and began scrubbing the sides. Frederick jumped up onto the edge of the tub watching as if he was calculating how many times she would scrub one spot before doing another.

She made sure he had plenty to eat and drink before packing his utensils. She had left the kennel close to his bedding on the floor and today she found him inside with one of his squeaking cat toys.

"I see you are ready to go, too," she said, closing the front gate to his kennel.

"Meow."

"I know you don't like to be locked up. But in a short while we will be at the airport and heading for the Moon."

She gathered her luggage about the time her comphone beeped. The view displayed a picture of her ex-husband. She closed the device and placed it in her pocket. She had been living alone for a few years and having no children, the divorce was quick and clean.

"Nothing will stop me now, not even you, Richard," she said, picking up the cat kennel.

Stepping out in the hallway she caught the next elevator going down. Alice deposited her apartment key at the front desk and walked out into the sunshine.

"This is going to be a great day, Frederick," she said placing him into her car. Taking a seat, she turned on the ignition, waited until the air car lifted up and retracted the wheel system to drive down the street.

Depositing her rental car at the airport, the airport autobus drove her off to the terminal she needed.

She checked in her largest luggage and showed the official her animal papers. After clearing security, she waited for the biggest step in her life.

Once on the shuttle, she secured the cat kennel by placing it under her seat. The kennel had soft walls inside

A. Nation

that would cushion the cat in the strong G force of the take off. About thirty passengers shared this craft with her. Within ten minutes, they were streaming through the clouds above toward the Moon.

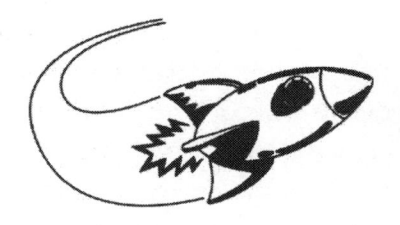

A. Nation

Moving On

A year and a half had passed. Frederick enjoyed the one-sixth gravity on the Moon especially when his human would open his cage and let him run–with leg weights, of course. They lived in a small protective structure tucked into a small crater not far from the mines joined by other community structures.

For the past year, his human would open the door to another human, he heard her call Matt. He was nice and let the cat stay on his lap. Then, the man stopped coming and now his mistress was filling a box with several of her skins she called clothes. He hopped up onto the single wide bed and walked over to paw her things from the open suitcase.

"Now, now," she admonished the feline as she removed his mid-body weighted wrap for his comfort, "You get to travel in your own case."

His ears perked up when a male voice sounded over the intercom, "Last call for those boarding ship for Mars. Please respond if you are scheduled to leave."

He watched her answer to the invisible person and then she reached over and removed his leg weights. Anticipating a run around the room, he was disappointed to be placed inside his kennel.

A. Nation

"Meow!" he demanded as the woman closed the wire door in front of him.

He watched as she closed her suitcase, pick up some papers, and hefted his cage off the bed. The door to the outer portion of the shelter opened and his cage was placed inside a larger container. There were two men sitting inside he hadn't recognized. Then the ground dropped out from beneath him as the vehicle flew up and away from the Moon's surface.

Once the shuttle stopped, one of the men helped his human with her luggage and lifted him up.

"You're taking this cat to Mars?" he asked.

"That's right. Thanks for your help," she said and located a cart to carry her load.

He could hear voices, lots of them as the wagon pulled him along. He looked around and remembered that he was here once before. The light gravity made him float within the cage.

"We'll wait here until our ship arrives. Oh, I bet this man will answer my question," she said.

All Frederick could understand was 'blah, blah, blah.'

He was dressed in green overalls and cap. Several badges on lanyards hung around his neck with an oxygen canister at his side.

"Are you ready to embark for Mars?" He questioned in his professional voice after he removed his mask to speak to her. His hologram epad tablet or Holopad, held in his right hand, was ready for inscription.

A. Nation

"Yes, do you know how long it might be? My schedule says 18:55 and it is now 18:32." Everyone on the Moon and Mars used the military time.

"The ship has arrived, but it will take about an hour to dock here and reload," he replied casually looking her over as men do when seeing a pretty woman. Then he heard it.

"Yeowwl"

"You have a cat?! Can you take a cat?" He exclaimed with surprise.

She reached for the papers stored in her insulated jacket.

"Yes, I can. Here is his permit and he has stayed with me for three years on the moon," Alice explained, presenting him the permits.

The two humans talked back and forth. Not caring about the encounter with the man, he curled up and drifted into a semi-sleep.

A loud voice, echoed across the terminal woke him up, and announced, "Passengers heading for Mars must board within the next thirty minutes."

"That's our ship," he heard Alice say as his kennel was picked up.

The same young man as before stood inside the fuselage's doorway, "Come here and I will carry your cat for you. So how long will you be on Mars?"

"Maybe two years, besides my work, I have a study I have been trying to complete," Alice replied as she followed the young man through ship's door. "Thank you for your help," she replied locating her assigned sitting area. She smiled and waved him on, then proceeded to put the cat crate under the couch.

As he tried to settle down again, another man walked over placing his dark colored shoes in front of his cage door.

"Alice Morgan, is it?" the man asked.

"Yes."

"I understand you have a cat with you. May I see your permits?" He stated without expression.

"Here, you will find all is in order," Alice noted, "and my cat has voided," she added.

Frederick fell back to sleep during this long monologue.

After a time, several people walked by his kennel until his mistress pulled out Frederick's cage, handed it to the waiting personnel, then reached for her own case to follow the officer through the ship's corridor. The next thing he saw, as she entered, was a small room.

"There you are Miss, if you need one of us, just press the red button on your call pad near the desk," he pointed with a smile.

"Thank you, I should be fine. Just place the cat in the corner." With that done, he left and closed the door behind him.

"Yeowwl!" Frederick cried, scratching the gate bars of his kennel.

A. Nation

"Okay, but let me disconnect the litter drawer first," she said.

He watched her slide a tray from beneath his cage and once that was out, she unlocked his kennel door.

He was ready to bolt out as fast as he could, but she caught him just as he was half out the cage door. She proceeded to strap on the body weight before letting him go.

Frederick surveyed the close quarters and did his business in the tray on the floor. The vibration from the turbines turning on aroused his senses. He looked around and didn't understand where the humming was coming from.

The lighter gravity allowed Alice to slip into her bed sack. He soon jumped up and joined her.

A. Nation

Mars

In the next three months, his routine consisted of food in the morning through a tube he would lick. Left alone for long periods of time locked in the small cabin, he would play with his squeaker and knock a few items to the floor from the nightstand. In the later hours before bedtime Alice would appear and feed him again.

At last, the ship entered the Martian orbit. Frederick was packed up again and hauled down to another level to exit the ship.

The airlocks between two metallic walls sounded with a loud 'clunk.' Frederick's ears twitched backward at the sudden noise. The call through the overhead sound system was announced to collect belongings and wait near the exit doors for embarking.

"Hear that, Frederick. It's time for us to go," his mistress said.

Everyone passed by until his human walked onto the shuttle. After they stepped through, the airlock slammed shut.

"Welcome aboard Miss Morgan, how was your flight?" an officer greeted.

"Very well, thanks. It was a smooth trip."

"Here, I will take your things and get you settled in your cabin. Oh, we have a cat, what is the name?" He inquired sincerely pulling up the cage to look inside.

"This is Frederick, an old pro at flying and living in space. He's very well behaved," Alice explained with a slight smirk.

The soldier caught the expression she gave and smiled back at her.

"Okay, this way," he gestured

Frederick rocked from side to side as his human carried him though a long hallway. When they arrived at their cabin, he sensed this room was larger than the last. His whiskers twitched at the colder temperature difference. He had received too many shots before leaving Earth and the Moon. One of them was to thicken his fur. His coat was thick and shiny as he licked it down.

He played with his squeaking toy when a man entered the cabin.

"Hi, I am Corporal Mark. Are you ready for the grand tour?" he beamed.

"Yes, let's get on with it," she said, rising and turning to put Frederick and his toy in his kennel.

He stared at the closed door, thinking she would return soon. When she didn't, he snuggled down into the soft blanket and dozed off.

After several days his mistress entered their cabin, closing the door behind her. She let him out and sat on the bed without moving. Frederick looked at her. He could tell there was something wrong. She kept repeating, "People are out there," in a soft low voice. He didn't understand her. After all, there are always people around them. But he knew she was worried about something.

Shivering, she picked him up and they sat huddled in the free standing chair available in the small room. After a few minutes, when she rose, he jumped down, and his mistress opened the desk drawer. Finding a small package, she tore open the top and poured the brown powder in a cup.

"There is a saying," she told the cat, as she stood up reaching for the packaged mix. "When all else fails, have chocolate!" Frederick just looked at her, sitting straight near the chair as he flicked his tail hoping for a treat.

Noticing the commotion had calmed outside in the hallway, he jumped up onto the bed with his toy. Alice was sitting in her straight back chair, when she leaned back and drank the last delicious drop of chocolate in the covered cup. Frederick looked up and twisted his ears toward the knock at the door. His mistress looked at him and then called out.

"Come in."

"Miss Morgan, may I come in?" Mike asked half way through the doorway.

"Yes, take this chair," she motioned getting up, offering hers, and sat on the edge of the bed.

"Miss Morgan—"

A. Nation

"Please call me Alice, Mike," she interrupted with a smile.

Frederick began licking the fur on his back when he saw the man pass over a sheet of paper to Alice.

After she looked the page over, she set it beside her on the bed. Frederick took a few steps and sniffed the thin sheet.

"Thanks, Mike, this job could help me out as well. I am also one of those confused people."

"You don't mind, do you?"

"Oh, no, I can emphasize with the rest of the people in this station and talking out our feelings will help us cope better, whatever happens."

He hesitated and stood up, nodded in agreement, and just barely mustered a "good-bye," as he opened the cabin door and left. Alice smiled at his obvious response to her relaxed clothing attire.

Frederick, still on the bed, was 'talking' to his squeaky toy that sounded like mews and whispered growls as he batted the shredded stuffed ball around.

"Come, Frederick." She reached for the flexible cat placing him in his kennel.

"Into your cage you go."

"Yeow."

"Yes, he was kind of funny wasn't he? But I'd better be careful with someone of his position. Supers are not a good idea for socializing." She said from past experience as if he understood.

A. Nation

Inside his cage, Frederick walked around in circles until he felt the bedding had the perfect indentation for easing himself down. He stared at her with his wide lime colored eyes. He tried to talk to her mind but nothing he did worked.

Alice stuffed his toy through the cage bars and then pulled out her uniform jumpsuit from the narrow closet along with her cap. She gathered up her ID badge and left her cabin for work, auto-locking the door as she left. After a minute, Frederick hypnotized stare flickered for a nanosecond as he settled down for his nap. Soon the days returned to a familiar routine.

Frederick, twisted around, was grooming his back on the bed when the door of Alice's cabin opened. The sound caused him to jerk for a second.

"Oh, Frederick, you never guess in a million years…" Alice went on describing her talk with someone named Emel and her encounter with Mike. Frederick only heard "blah, blah, blah, blah…," and proceeded to continue his grooming since he didn't hear the word 'food' or 'kibble' mentioned. He soon noticed that his mistress did not come over and scratch behind his ears as she usually does. She sat at her desk tapping on a machine that also went "blah, blah, blah." He then jumped off the bed and onto the desk. Alice stretched out her left hand, but just patted the top of his head, he didn't care for that.

"Yeoowww!"

A. Nation

"I'm sorry, Freddy, but I got to get this done first while it is still fresh in my mind, then we'll have a hot chocolate and treat time." Energized, Alice continued to transcribe her notes. For a second the cat's ears pricked upward at the mention of 'treat;' but when Alice's attention moved away from him, he decided to take his frustrations out on his squeaky mouse toy by a flying attack to the floor.

The next day Frederick heard the door being unlatched and jumped down from the bed. Sitting close to the door, he saw it open with his mistress standing in the doorway. He wanted to know what was that place behind her filled with more human sounds.

"Scoot! Back inside!" she exclaimed, waving her free hand toward the inside of her cabin and then closed the door. From her left arm, she placed her notes near her computer upon the small metal desk. Frederick wanting attention jumped up upon the desk and sat on Alice's notepad.

"Okay, Freddy, you will have to get down now. I've got work to do."

Extracting the notebook out from Frederick's posterior put the cat off balanced, causing him to jump off the desk. Alice then threw his squeaky toy to the floor, hoping that would distract him. The toy bounced on the small rug covering the tiled floor near the bed and rolled under the narrow nearby nightstand. It came to a stop on a small screw of the ventilator screen near the bed frame. When Frederick caught up with the toy, he found after a few scratches that the toy had stuck to the screw. After whapping it several times, he realized that he couldn't dislodge it. Frederick looked at Alice, but because humans can't read cat minds, he batted it a few more times. He decided to hop on the bed and proceeded to wash his tail. The toy remained dangling on the loose screw.

Every day his human would disappear in the morning and return at night. He wanted to know where she was going.

The next couple of days, Frederick tried to scratch his squeaky toy off of the loosened air vent. Then he heard the cabin door click to open. Quickly he got onto the bed, flicking his tail back and forth betraying his excitement.

"Oh, Freddy, have you been a good boy?"

Frederick just gazed at her. Humans always have to use their mouths for more noise, but he did recognize his name when called.

"I'm sorry Mister, but I'd better put you in your kennel." Picking up the large flexible cat, she brought him to the cage and guided him to enter.

"Yeow," Frederick protested.

Alice grabbed up her notepad, and quipped upon leaving, "I'll be back later. Just have yourself a good snooze." With that, she latched the cage and walked out to begin her day of work.

Frederick turned around three or four times to finally get settled. He stared with contempt at the cabin door, hoping his mistress would return soon; but then after a few minutes, he gave up and decided that licking his forepaws was more important at this time.

It was one of those days when Alice returned to the cabin and let Frederick out of his cage. He watched her remove her skins and step into the toilet room. The shower began running. He could feel sorry for the human having no hair for warmth but that thought passed fast. The cat wondered why humans can't just lick themselves clean. Getting bored he jumped down to the twenty-four inch air vent screen to bat his toy about. The toy still would not release from the screw from which it hung. Every time Frederick pawed at the small object, the screen screw of the vent loosened, and then suddenly it popped off onto the floor.

Frederick bent down to smell the small screw, and deciding it wasn't edible, he turned his attention toward the air vent. As he began to pull the aluminum screen toward him, he found it could bend toward him, leaving a small opening where he could hear voices. *'Maybe there is food down there,'* he thought. Luckily his mistress had removed his body weight, leaving the small ankle weights on. His bulky size almost didn't fit, but cats with their limber spine are able to rotate until… he vanished down the ventilation shaft!

Frederick strolled, sometimes skidded, through the smooth aluminum vent shaft. Hearing voices, he stopped to listen. The maintenance crew had begun their supper time. Frederick licked his whiskers with one broad sweep to the right, then the left.

He let out a "Yeow," but the men were loudly playing some musical instrument. Someone near this particular vent asked if they heard anything unusual, only to get a "What?" response over the din of the music. So off he went.

He had been walking for some time through this tube container until light appeared up ahead. Frederick pawed the grate but it wouldn't give. Different voices could be heard as he pawed again at the stubborn metal bars, and then he yowled out.

The people across the room jumped up as soon as they heard the strange throaty howl that seemed to echo throughout the room. The people stopped eating and looked at each other when he emitted a louder howl from the air vent.

First, Frederick scratched the grate. Then he bumped his head against the barrier and burst through the quarters. The people jumped up and on their sitting divan. Frederick jumped up as well into a small nearby chair.

He could smell their fear as they raised their hands. Frederick hissed and spread his fur outward, causing his bushy appearance to look even larger. Then he noticed the uneaten sandwich on the floor, he calmed down and proceeded to take a few big bites.

Other people came to the open door and looked down at him. They said something but like the humans, their words were only 'blah, blah, blah.'

A. Nation

Before he knew it, two cloth covered people entered on all fours until one of them scooped him up. He flung out his claws at them but couldn't reach their body as they held their long arms straight out. The other covered person held up a cloth and wrapped it around Frederick until he could fight no more.

"Take this one to the lab," said one of them.

He soon found himself in a glass enclosure with holes for air. While he stuck one white paw threw an air hole, the strangers turned on a bright light and injected something into his tail. The lights faded and the next time he was awake, his mistress was taking possession of his carrier.

"Oh, you naughty boy!" Alice exclaimed and then to the ahman she proclaimed, "Thank you so much, I am so very sorry this has happened."

"Not to worry, once the hysterics were calmed down, we knew what to do. I hope you don't mind, but we had to make a thorough study of the animal to make sure it was disease free. A small biopsy was taken from the tip of its tail." The ahman explained pointing to a tiny bald spot on the end of the cat's furry self.

Alice, unsure by what they did, took the container and replied with hesitation, "Thank you again." With urgency, Mike and Alice left the airlock and drove back overland.

A. Nation

Keeping Warm

Conservation of energy was of prime importance in the human's Mars base during the solar cell shutdowns. Storage batteries would last about a half day. Most personnel left their insulated suits on when sleeping in their cabins to keep warm. Solar panels are useful when the sun can energize them, but today no heat could be produced and the backup batteries were losing power. Emergency hydrogen and methane turbines did the work for the basic needs of lighting and the computers. Alice had returned to her cabin with a cold sandwich.

She wrapped another cloth around Frederick's body weight halter.

"Here, Freddy, I am going to cover your kennel, but for now, I'm going to let you out to warm up my bed," Alice said aloud to the blank stares of the cat.

"Yeow!" he replied as his ears twitched in all directions feeling the nippy air.

At that moment, a knock came on the cabin door. Frederick watched from the bed to see who it might be.

"Yes?" She called.

"It's me, Mike, can I come in?" The voice asked.

"Yes," she responded, clicking on an object, he had once knocked off the stand by her bed.

"Uh, since keeping warm is a priority, a bunch of us are congregating in the cafeteria. It is a lot warmer there. Want to come?"

"Can I take Frederick?" Alice asked as the cat quickly poked his head out of the bed sack to see who else was in the room.

"You bet, uh, let me get his cage for you."

Gathering up a couple of extra blankets and Frederick, they both left the cold cabin behind.

The cafeteria was warmer than the cabin. Alice set the kennel down on the floor. A couple of people and a child came over to investigate the cat inside. Mike left their corner as Alice allowed him to come out of his carrier with his halter attached.

One day, while his human was gone, Frederick jumped on the bed and down to the floor to play with his squeaker toy. She returned at lunchtime to change her clothes.

He pawed at the closed door.

"No, you're not going out. In fact, just to make sure, I think you better stay in your cage until dinner time," he heard her voice.

All he could make out was "No.......dinner time." He struggled a bit when Alice pushed him into the kennel. He didn't like staying there all day.

"I'll let you out tonight, bye," she said.

Later that afternoon, his cage shook for a few minutes. Alice still hadn't returned to the cabin.

"Yeow," he demanded.

Soon lights dimmed and he fell asleep.

The next morning a strange woman entered the cabin, closing the door behind her.

"I'll bet you're hungry and have to go," the older woman said.

"I'm Leona, your Alice will be back in no time."

"Yeow?"

The heavy set lady searched the desk drawer and found a can of cat food. She emptied in into Frederick's bowl and then unlatched his kennel door.

He watched her and jumped out of the cage to do his business on the floor tray.

"You just take your time. I'll wait until you eat your food. You are probably wondering why I'm here and not your owner. Well, she was in an accident, but now she's recovering just fine. That was a scare for all of us when that tunnel caved in," she said.

Frederick didn't care, as long as he had some food to eat.

"That's a good kitty. You ate it all. I'm afraid I'll have to put you back into your kennel. Will you let me?"

Leona started to reach down and pick up the large cat but he dodged her and decided the safety of the kennel was better for him.

"Good boy," she said, latching the door gate.

"I'll let her know I took care of you. Bye Bye," she said and left the cabin.

Frederick stared at the door after the woman left and laid down still looking out of his cage door.

Late in the next morning, Frederick woke up when the cabin door opened. His mistress was leaning on a long stick while a man in white clothing helped her to the bed.

"I think I can be okay now, thank you," she said.

"All right, but don't hesitate to call us, if you need help," the medic said.

Oh, can you let my cat out? Just make sure he doesn't follow you when you leave.

"Sure," he said, unlatching the cage door.

Frederick hesitated and then jumped out and sprung up onto Alice's bed.

He watched her for a few minutes as she resettled herself higher onto the bed to sit up against the wall. Satisfied she would be all right, he turned and left the cabin.

Frederick snuggled up to his mistress and began to purr.

"Aw, you did miss me," she said stroking his back fur.

Stretching over to her night stand, she pulled an etablet out to read her book. After an hour, she fell asleep.

When she awoke, she knew she had to get up.

"Come on, Freddy, I have to get up," she said, swinging the good leg over the edge of the bed and holding onto her repaired leg. "I got to go…"

She grabbed her cane and after a few steps at a time, she made it to the toilet room.

Returning was just as strenuous until she sat on the edge of the bed and pushed herself with her good leg to a more comfortable position. Frederick curled up at her feet. Her door chimed and before she could press the remote to open the door, Leona walked in carrying what looked like a tray of food.

"Mmm, that smells good," Aliced said, smiling.

"I figured you wouldn't be walking around the cafeteria, so I brought you lunch."

"You're the best. I heard you took care of Frederick last night. Thank you."

"Has Frederick had his meal of the day?" Leona asked.

"Not yet."

"Well, you just eat and I'll take care of that."

Frederick watched as the woman from yesterday pulled out another can of cat food.

"Yeow."

Leona stayed a while until Alice finished eating. When Alice pushed the food tray away, her friend picked up the platter and left the cabin.

"Well, there's not much to do, Frederick, is there?" she said.

A sudden knock sounded on her cabin door. The abrupt noise startled Frederick, who ran into his cage and peered back out.

A. Nation

"Come in!" she shouted, not wanting to get up, as she pressed the 'unlock' remote button near her bedside.

"Just I," Mike revealed as the steel door opened. "I thought I would check to see how you were doing."

"Just fine, but I am bored out of my mind. You know they won't even let me talk to my ahman contact, Emel. What is going on?"

Mike took a seat on the only chair in the room. "Remember that soldier that was in your infirmary room asking you questions?"

"Yes, what was that about?"

"There has been an incident and we are starting an investigation."

"Mike, what is it?" She replied with impatience.

"An ahman assigned to one of my work crews before the tunnel breach has been found dead. It looks like someone did it in."

"Oh, that's terrible. What's being done? You said someone, do you know who?"

"We are just assembling the investigating team of humans and ahmans, so would you like to be on our team?" He sat with his hands folded between his legs, waiting for her to say something as he looked at her.

"Me? Well…Yes. At least, it's something I can do." She expressed placing her reading tablet down nearby onto the bed.

"Good, I will let you know what time and where we will be meeting. It should be today or tomorrow. Is there anything I can get you for now? Is Mr. Frederick behaving himself?"

"No, I don't need anything now, but thanks for filling me in about this and the invite. Frederick is staying put now since the vent screen was fixed."

Mike looked briefly around her small cabin, "Good, I will call you as soon as we set a meeting date." Mike then stood up and left the room shutting the door behind him.

Frederick stared at the closing door and back to Alice. She reached over to his toy he had brought up onto the bed and gave it a throw. Even with the body weights his jump was higher than usual. Alice began to laugh.

A. Nation

Weeks Later

Lying on her bed, Alice threw Frederick's squeaky toy to the floor just to watch him chase it down. When a knock came upon her cabin door, she rose and walked over to let Mike in.

"Are you busy? He asked.

"Are you kidding? Come on in," Alice motioned toward the solitary chair in the room.

"I'm glad the trial is over. Come here Freddy Boy," he said as he greeted the large cat. Frederick just sat and stared at him. "I just got the word; you can sit in on the next interview."

"Really? Well, that's great Mike. I hope our actions concerning Jay Simmons sent a message to all of our people that violence isn't the answer to prejudice."

Frederick returned to his spot on the end of the bed and decided the noisy humans were not giving him any food in the near future. He started grooming himself until the humans came falling onto the bed sending Frederick leaping off to the floor.

He watched them for just a moment looking at each other, when suddenly they heard the man's phone ring. He pulled the com device out, studied it, and rose to a sitting position. Frederick jumped back onto the bed as Alice also sat up.

The man known as Mike said more to his mistress and then leaned down to kiss her on the mouth with a deep embrace.

Disturbed again, "Yeow," Frederick protested.

Breathless, she squeaked out, "That sounds good. Mike, I have to get ready for work too. Have you heard when the next interview will be held with the aliens?" She queried, still flushed by his kiss as she followed him to her door.

"I will let you know as soon as I find out," he said leaving the room.

A few weeks later, Frederick watched his human talk to the window on her desk. Jumping onto the edge of the small desk he saw a person's face talking back. Then his mistress said, "Well, I will let you go and talk to you later."

She turned off the com connection and turned around in her chair to address the cat, "Well, Frederick, that was news," she remarked. "Meeia had a baby. Funny how our preconceived decisions didn't think that strong one would have a child.

Frederick was busy licking his paw for a head wash. As soon as Alice spoke, he stopped momentarily to stare at her, not understanding a thing she said. After hearing 'blah, blah, blah,' he resumed his fastidious cleaning process.

A. Nation

Alice got up to get some hot chocolate mix when her console beeped aloud indicating a message. A communique sent by the Major requested her presence as soon as possible.

"Freddy, my boy, I will have to take off, so into your cage you go."

"Yeow," the cat protested.

"I know, but duty calls and I just don't trust you."

She placed the cat with care into the cage and latched it. She then gathered up her work epad, locking the door behind her as she left the cabin.

Frederick's routine didn't alter much during the next few weeks. Once in a while he was allowed to go with her to the library leashed. He enjoyed the change of scenery and when a stranger petted him too much, he would jump up into Alice's lap under her reader.

Mike visited their cabin often and Frederick liked the scraps of chicken he brought. Today, her cabin door was open, when the man appeared. Frederick was on his leash playing with his new rat toy Leona had made. When Mike entered, Frederick licked his whiskers in anticipation of the morsels to come.

"Hey," he said closing the door behind him.

"Hey yourself, what's up?" Alice asked.

The cat received the food scrap from Mike and listened to their conversation with disinterest.

Another day passed, when Alice ran into their cabin.

A. Nation

"I have to hurry, Freddy. I'll let you out long enough for you to eat," she said, rummaging around in the desk drawer for another can of cat food. Peeling off the lid, she scooped out the contents into his food bowl.

"I'll give you ten minutes and then I'll have to leave. Eat up."

He looked at the food and up at his mistress for nine of those minutes. When he noticed her foot tapping, he sniffed and ate most of the moist food. By the time he had finished, Alice had left the cabin.

~*CrossRoads A Moment of Decision*~

A year had gone by in a regular routine with Alice was sitting on the bed writing on her epad and Frederick, also on the bed, pawing at his fuzzy rat toy. Mike entered the cabin.

"You don't have a shift at this hour?" He asked her.

"No, I was relieved by my replacement, so I came back here to message Jennifer. What about you?" Alice asked as he sat on the bed beside her.

"I'm still in charge of the labor pool until we leave. There should be someone arriving in a few days so I can show him or her the layout." Mike sat down beside her.

Alice rose onto her knees to face Mike's back and began massaging his shoulders. Fredrick came over and decided to do the same on Mike's arm, purring as he pressed one front paw then the other.

A. Nation

"Frederick you are going to have to stay in your kennel," Mike said picking up the fat cat and placing him inside the cage.

The cat saw Mike turn and lean over Alice to give her a kiss as they both fell back on the bed. Frederick, annoyed that he had been taken out of his comfort zone to his cage, was not happy and began pawing the inside of the kennel. They ignored him.

Mike's comphone rang. "Don't answer it," she whispered

"I have to, it's the Major. He wants both of us in his office."

"Why is it when we start to have some time together, the Major calls? Does he have bugs in this room?" she asked pretending to look around.

"I hope not. Come, let's go and we can pick up afterward."

"All right," she said putting her black boots on. "It will seem odd not being with the others when we get to Earth."

"Yeah, that is why we should keep in touch," he mused, opening the cabin door for her.

Frederick just stared at the closing door.

Two weeks had passed by and today was the day those returning to Earth began packing their personal belongings for the long trip.

A. Nation

Frederick watched from his kennel, his human folded her blue Mylar suit and placed it with care into her suitcase. A few other items, like a comb, hairbrush, toothbrush, and lotion, were placed into a small bag. Frederick's toys and enough packaged food for three months were stacked into a separate carrying case from her clothing suitcase. He recalled a scene like this before.

"Are you ready Alice?" Mike asked.

"Yes, just one more thing," she said as she opened all the drawers and cupboards to make sure nothing was left.

"OK, I'm ready," she announced reaching for Frederick's kennel handle on top.

"Here, let me take him," Mike offered, reaching for the cage before she could. Frederick emitted soft growling noises.

"Don't mind him. He doesn't like to be shifted around when carried," Alice remarked as they continued down the hallway.

"He'll get used to it," he replied.

The clatter of people talking and walking excited Frederick. At the same time the noise scared him. He never seen this many people in one place before.

About an hour later, Mike and Alice opened their new accommodations on the returning ship to Earth. The cabin was smaller than his human's single Mars cabin, but this one had a larger sleeping area for two people. A large desk was noticed snug against the padded wall with cupboards above. A computer monitor was set flush with the wall that could pull out to use. The toilet was just to their left with a small sink, and the bed sacks hung by the cupboards along the wall.

"Oh, put Frederick over in the corner there and I will take this side of the desk," she decided.

They stayed a while, let Frederick have a run around the compartment, and then he noticed Alice had disappeared.

Mike started throwing Frederick's squeaker around for him to chase. Later Alice returned and she didn't look too happy.

"Careful, he might take a bite out of your hand," Alice warned, sitting by the limited desktop still stewing about something.

Mike gave Frederick his toy and continued speaking to her.

"You look deep in thought, Alice, is anything the matter?"

"No, I mean yes. Did you know Mathew Miller was on board this ship?"

He sat up, "Yes, he became one of my laborers after he got fired from the Lasswitz Crater mine."

"You didn't think to tell me?"

Frederick sensed a tension in the room and jumped up into Alice's lap.

"I thought you were over him?" He asked.

A. Nation

"I am. I just don't like being blind sighted. I ran into him at the commissary." Frederick's mistress gave him a couple of strokes on this back.

"And?" Mike stood up by her.

"Oh, we just said hello, and I told him to not to interfere with our lives. Then I just walked away."

Mike put his arms around her, "I guess I should have let you know. But with the packing and turning over my work crew to another super was all I could think of at the time."

She stood up as he circled his arms around her.

"You're excused, Mr. Carone, what say we go get lunch?" she queried feeling the warmth in his arms.

Mike turned to pick up Frederick and scooted him into the caged kennel.

A. Nation

Earth

The flight back from Mars took forty-two days. Frederick was just getting into the routine of things when an announcement from the overhead cabin announcement let everyone know they could now disembark. Alice removed his cramped body weights, allowing him to feel more flexible. Then the sensation of his cage lifting up bothered him until he felt pulled down to the ground.

His ears perked around when a loud metal scraping noise could be heard as attendants outside prepared their exit. When the tall eight-foot hatch door slid open to the left of the portal, the exhaling of cabin pressure commenced.

One by one the passengers began disembarking down to the concourse of the terminal through the enclosed pressurized ramp that allowed their bodies to adjust to Earth's gravity. Some still had to be helped by service attendants or 'walk-along' robots to help steady those still weaken by the heavier pressure.

His kennel was set on the floor in the terminal. The people strolling by his kennel stimulated his senses. Having a hard time standing, he began to howl.

A. Nation

"Calm down, Freddy, we're almost there," he heard Alice say.

Once again his kennel was lifted up and taken outside. The brightness hurt his eyes but the smell invoked memories from long ago. He could hear the birds chirp and the busy vehicles driving by. The humans loaded him into a larger human container and climbed inside with him.

He slept some in the car until he heard his name mentioned.

"Yes, we were going to drive north to visit relatives, not sure if we will take the land shuttle or drive as we have Frederick. So, Alex, why are you in Phoenix?" Mike inquired to the other human walking alongside.

"Just over another case, say since you are heading my way, why don't you come and stay a while at my home? My car is parked outside."

"Well, uh…" Mike started to say.

"Who's up north?" the other man asked.

"My parents live in Idaho and then we were going on to see Alice's cousin in Grand Junction, Colorado."

"You could leave Frederick with us; we would take real good care of him."

"I know you would, I'm not sure, and we haven't met Jan yet. Is she still with you?" Alice asked.

"Yes, in fact, we got married a few months ago."

"Congratulations." Alice and Mike replied.

A. Nation

Later during the drive when the car stopped, Alice clipped on Frederick's halter and guided him to a grassy spot near a parking lot. After some time, she picked him up before he could climb one of the tree trunks. She guided him into his kennel and latched the gate.

Then they stopped again. The air was dusty and the wind was blowing. Frederick heard a new voice.

"So good to meet you," the new female voice remarked catching her breath from the hug Alex had given her. Then she spotted the carrying case for Alice's cat. Alex began explaining.

"Alice has a cat and I thought the ride would be a better choice than taking the shuttle."

"A cat. Better be careful around our dog, Ralph. He acts before he thinks," Jan warned.

"Frederick is in a kennel, and if we introduce him while he is in his cage, they can smell each other."

"Ralph needs a bath, Alex. That is why he's not coming inside. He took a roll in the desert."

Alex noted the restriction and waved his friends inside. "Come in, we have plenty of room for you."

Up the porch steps they walked as the large head of a dog sniffed everyone going by. Frederick saw the animal first. Ralph got the whiff of something familiar in one of Alice's containers.

"A cat? Oh boy, I love chasing cats," the dog woofed.

"Buzz off, dog. Come near me and you will go blind," warned Frederick as he was hauled into the house.

A. Nation

He pawed his kennel door. Then he heard his mistress say something.

"Mike, I'm going to take Frederick out for a walk. Since the dog is tied up, I'll go over by the barn," Alice explained as he felt the kennel rising again.

"Maybe when you return, give Ralph another smell of your cat," Jan offered.

When Alice opened the door, she could see that Jan had tied the now shortened rope to the porch support. Ralph stood up as soon as he saw the kennel in her hand, but he could not get close enough to peek inside.

"Hisssssss!"

"Now Frederick, we are going to have to get along here. I will let you out behind the barn. If you go near Ralph, you go at your own risk," Alice explained as if her cat understood.

"Yeow."

Alice hauled the kennel as her feet kicked up the dusty sand from the barren ground.

"Yes, life is tough. Here's a good spot." Alice placed the kennel down on the sandy surface and opened the kennel door with care.

Frederick jolted and then stopped. He wasn't used to wearing his leg and body weights anymore which now gave him a little more flexibility even in this new gravity. Frederick first looked out and realized that he could leave with abandon. With one paw then the next, touching the sandy soil, he crept out of the cage and walked over to an edge of creosote bushes, squatted, and then he ran.

"Frederick! Come back!"

The cat tore around the barn, *"I'm free!"* Then he saw the dog.

Ralph had now perked up and scrambled down the porch only to be jerked backward by the rope attached to his collar.

"Freddy!" Alice called running after her cat.

By now Ralph was barking and whining but his rope jerked him just beyond the last step. Frederick had stopped two feet from him and stretched a foot closer.

"What are you yapping about, you, you hairy animal?"

"Chase, chase, I gotta chase you (gag)."

"I can slice and dice you in seconds you flea bit mongrel. Hissssss"

"I'll get you cat," he barked.

Frederick stretched as much as he dared toward the dog, *"Yeah, you and who else?"*

"If I wasn't tied up..."

"And do what? I'll tell you dog, first I'll scratch your eyes out, and then I'll rip off your silly nose. Back off!"

Ralph proceeded to bark many more times, *"Let me get my teeth around you cat."*

"That's Frederick to you, mutt," he responded arching his back and displaying a full spread of fur standing out in all directions to make himself look even larger.

Frederick noticed his human returning to the home.

Ralph gave the cat one of his signature loud barks. His master stepped out onto the porch and admonished him as Alice returned into the house.

"Ralph sit," the man ordered in a low booming voice, "you behave. I don't want to hear you every time that cat gets near you. Understand?"

Ralph's ears drooped a half inch as he sat panting with his tongue out. Frederick watched as the dog looked at his master and then him. Ralph stood up and started wiggling in his excitement but the large man pressed his rear back down.

"You got them trained well, dog," Frederick mewed.
"My name is Ralph, but when do I get to chase you?"
"Even if you did you wouldn't catch me."

"OK you two," Alice said as she picked up Frederick and headed back to the barn where the kennel had been left.

Everyone headed back inside when Alice returned into the home with Frederick inside the cage.

How long can you stay and where will your travels take you next?" Jan asked.

"We can only stay a few days, then we'll head north to see his parents and over to Colorado to visit my cousin," Alice related opening the kennel door for Frederick, who sniffed around and then hopped onto the couch near Alice. "Frederick, not all people want you on their furniture."

"That's all right, and it's old. I haven't told Alex yet that I have ordered a new set to modernize this room a little."

A. Nation

"You know I would have never in my life believed that I would be living in this desert."

Jan turned and sat on the couch with Frederick between them. Alice scratched behind Frederick's ears as he leaned into her fingernails.

The next morning, Frederick sauntered into the main living area to check his food bowl. Finding nothing, Frederick lapped a drink from the water dish and jumped up onto Jan's sofa.

"Frederick is a little grouchy right now, I should take him outside soon, but as you can see, he'd rather lay on your couch. If you don't want him there, just say so," he heard Alice say with little understanding other than his name was mentioned.

Alice picked up the heavy cat and guided him into his cage. Without another word, she walked out onto the porch passing Ralph who was lying by the steps. He picked up his head and noticed the cage with increase excitement.

"Cat?"

"Hissss! Dog are you still here?"

"Now you two cut that out," Alice reprimanded walking down the wooden steps. "We're going over here Freddy," she said speaking to the cat as if he understood.

Carrying the kennel to the far side of the house, she set it down on the dirt and opened it.

A. Nation

Frederick stepped out and walked within distance of Ralph's restraint. The two animals began discussing their territorial rules when they both heard a funny sound from the barn.

Frederick turned his head and back to Ralph, *"What was that?"*

"Another animal, I wasn't allowed to see."

"Well I will, stay here dog," the cat commanded, turning to go.

"Mistress calls me Ralph."

"Whatever."

The main double doors on the barn were open as the cat peeked into the darkness by the door's edge.

"Eh-eh-eh-eh-Bah! Who goes there, friend or foe?"

Frederick looked up at the white animal with horns, which appeared to be tied to a stall post. *"What kind of animal are you?"*

"I am a goat, don't get close. My horns are lethal."

"Well I'm a cat, you can call me Frederick. What do you do?"

"I give milk, can you?"

"No, I kill vermin."

"Ewwwww."

"Now that dog out there, who knows what he does?"

"Dog, did you say dog? Help, there's a wolf out there, help."

"Shut up you fool, do you want the humans to come running? That dog couldn't do much, he's tied like you are."

A. Nation

Calming down, the goat showed the cat the chewed off the piece of the rope that was tied to the stall. *"Oh yeah?"*

"I think I'll leave you goat."

"That's Carmelia to you cat."

"Frederick."

"Whatever."

Backing out so his backside wouldn't present a target to the goat and her horns, Frederick strolled back to Ralph.

"Well?"

"Just a goat."

"What's a goat?" Ralph asked sitting now on the porch.

"It's an animal with horns on its head and it says it gives milk."

"You're making this up right?"

"No, now what do you do besides bark all the time?"

"I save people."

"Doing what, scaring them with your bark?"

"I saved my mistress from a bad man. I crawled out this window see and jumped on him. Oh what fun that was," Ralph related when an intruder tried to hurt Jan.

"I guess that could be useful. I can jump on people too," Frederick forewarned displaying his front right claws.

"Okay cat, er, Frederick, and if that goat comes out, you can jump on it."

"Naw, I don't care about animals with horns."

"Once I almost got in trouble when I ran up to a buck in the hills before coming here."

A. Nation

"*I have been to the Moon and Mars,*" Frederick began as he stepped closer to the dog.

"*Get out, cats can't go there. What's there anyway?*"

"*Nothin' no trees, no grass, no birds, no…*"

"*Wait, why did you go?*"

"*My human servant worked there–same thing on Mars.*"

"*That sounds awful, did you get to run about?*"

"*No, but I did have fun running through the air ducts on Mars and finding more people.*"

"*What is Mars?*"

"*A desert world like Earth.*"

"*Who are the extra people?*"

"*Nice people and scared of me, that's a good thing.*"

"*Any other animals there?*"

"*No, but Alice showed me a kitten, said it was from me. I don't know how that happened without my knowledge.*"

"*That is strange. I'm tired,*" Ralph muttered lying back down on the porch.

Frederick, being a nocturnal animal, was tired of all this talking. As soon as the dog laid down on his bedding, Frederick crept closer and curled up on the rumpled blanket.

With the door open to catch the cool breezes, Frederick heard his name mentioned from inside the house. Stretching, he walked in where the two human women were talking.

"*–think what is best for Frederick. He will be okay here won't he?*"

A. Nation

She took a deep breath and in a moment of decision, "Okay, but only if you would message me each day so I don't have to worry much about him?"

"I will, he'll be fine until you come back." Frederick hearing his name poked his head up to peer at the two women.

"We fly out of Denver but maybe Mike can change the tickets or we will just come back here."

"Or we can meet you, please don't worry. He'll be all right here."

The next day, Frederick wasn't even paying attention to his humans when they left the house. By the evening, he noticed they weren't around. Instead, this new human they called Jan was still here. A few days had passed when Frederick noticed this Jan person was putting clothing into a suitcase. He stepped into the luggage.

"Out, out, you will get your own carrying case," she scolded, shooing the cat away.

The next thing he knew, he and his kennel were placed in the back of a vehicle. After a short drive, Jan took him on a shuttle where he fell asleep. When the craft landed in a cooler location she called Montrose, Colorado, she carried him into a house with many food smells. Alice set him and his kennel in a bedroom.

Hector, the resident dachshund, knew something was amiss. He could tell there was a new smell in the house after the company left. Alice's bedroom door was ajar. With a nose here and a paw there, he pried the door open and headed for the kennel at the end of the bed.

"What are you?" the dog asked.

"Hisssss. Beware dog or you shall go blind." Frederick was not in the mood for this silly little animal. He wanted to get out of this container.

"See here cat, this is my house. I won't have you being insolent to me," he yipped.

Frederick just turned around and stared at Hector over his black shoulder.

"It looks like they are already getting to know each other. I'm sorry Freddy, let's take you outside for some exercise," Alice said to him.

She picked up the kennel with Frederick and headed for the back door. The other woman, Alice called Andrea followed close behind. Hector was at their heels.

She placed the kennel on the patio tiles outside of the kitchen door. Hector got in close to the gate to get a firsthand look when his mistress, Andrea, pulled his collar to get him out of the way.

Alice opened the gate a half-inch at a time until Frederick's head poked through the opening. Andrea pulled her dog away allowing about eight feet between the wiggling canine and the cat emerging.

Hector barked, "Let's play."

Frederick shimmied passed the gate before Alice could catch him. Hector gave chase.

A. Nation

At first, the feline stood his ground staring at the humans and that noisy short dog. Frederick turned and hissed at Hector.

Hector motioned toward the cat when he heard a 'hisssss' and saw that Frederick was growing in size with his teeth barred.

"Come any closer and you die shorty."

"I just want to play." Hector danced around the crouching cat. *"What are you, what's your name?"*

"I-am-a-cat! Frederick is my name." The feline walked over to the edge of the garden where the rose bushes reside and did his business in the soft soil. He then relaxed some and sat up with less of his hair sticking out. He judged the animal before him couldn't be much of a threat due to the dog's short stature."

"I am Hector, a full pedigree, over ten generations dachshund. A dog!" He yipped with proudness in his voice.

Frederick took a step forward stretching his tail into the air. *"I'll just call you Hiccup,"* he decided and sauntered toward the grassy yard.

"Hey, it's Hector, and where are you going? Why are you here?" The dog barked.

Frederick strolled back and came face to face and nose to nose from the dog's wet black nostril. Andrea held her hand to her mouth.

"I don't know why I'm here, but you better not get in my way," Frederick growled.

A. Nation

The dog sneezed and danced around, *"Ok, wanna race?"*

Recovering from the nose spray, Frederick wiped his face with his paw. *"You're on."*

At first, they took off together, but the cat's strengthen muscles from running in the Arizona desert, and improved agility out maneuvered Hector. Toward the end of their race, Frederick leaped up into one of Andrea's maple trees.

"Hey, no fair," the dog barked as he jumped at the tree trunk and circled it several times. His short front paws patted the tree without success.

Frederick hopped up and sat on one of the lawn chairs near a chain link backed leaf hedge that lined Andrea's yard. He then stretched out positioning himself for a nice sunny rest only to be interrupted by a 'shush, shush, shush' noise.

Opening one eye then the next the black and white cat could see dirt flinging out from under the hedge.

"What are you doing, Heck?"

The little dog backed out and looked at Frederick.

"Digging," he barked and returned to his chore.

"I know that. Why?"

"There's a whole yard on the other side I can run around in."

"Ho hum," the cat meowed rolling over to his other side.

"Hector, Hector time to come in," he heard the dog's mistress call.

A. Nation

Distracted from his current endeavors, he raced inside hoping his food dish would be full. Frederick raised his head and watched the dachshund run passed. Not wanting to miss anything, he sprung off of the lawn chair and almost beat Hector through the kitchen doorway.

A week later, Frederick heard an exchange between the woman who lived here and her daughter.

Felicia asked her mother, "Why do I need to go? It's just a lot of old stuff." She wanted to go to the holo movies with her friends.

"The family that goes together stays together. Hush up and go see if your brother is ready." Her daughter rolled her eyes and took off for Jeffery's room.

"Where's everybody going? Can I go too?" Hector asked Frederick."

"No, and I'm not interested," the large cat said lying down on Hector's bed.

Hector fussed and whined around the cat trying to reclaim his bed while he avoided those sharp feline claws. When Frederick didn't move, the little dachshund curled up to the back side of the small bed and slumped in.

They could hear dishes rattling. Hector and Frederick rose out of their cloth bedding to see if their mistresses had any food.

The next day, Alice had been working with a wire fence from the house to the hedge. After both animals watched

A. Nation

Alice disappear around the corner into the house, Hector strutted over to his special digging spot beneath the foliage. Frederick took a bounding leap and landed on top of the squared off hedge.

"Hop up here and you can see everything," the cat taunted.

"Huh? I can't jump that high," Hector replied and returned to his digging.

"Well, I can." With a mighty leap, Frederick bounded off the seven-foot tall fence hedge. First he looked around and didn't see any humans, and then he returned to the neighbor's side of the fencing to agitate Hector.

"You'll never get over here," the cat teased.

"I'll get you cat. My nose found the bottom!" he barked.

"You can't get me, you can't get me."

Hector was getting tired but continued on until a small tunneled hole began to appear.

"See, I'm doing it."

By now he was 'gruffing' and growling as he made the hole larger. He was able to squeeze his head in but backed up when he decided he couldn't get his wide shoulders through. After another kick of dirt behind his back legs, he wiggled under the chain link fence only to scratch himself on one of the exposed wires.

"Yiiiii," he yelped.

"Shut up you fool, do you want the humans to hear you?"

"(Sniff) but it hurts."

A. Nation

Frederick came around and checked his back. *"I only see a little scratch. It's not even bloody. You are such a wimp."*

"Really, wow look at this yard."

Both of them raced around the manicured yard inspecting all of the corners when they heard Hector's mistress scream.

"Come on, we don't want them to find your secret escape," Frederick mewed. He then led the dog out of the fence by stretching up to the latch. When it fell Frederick pulled the gate door open into the yard.

"Just come with me and look innocent."

They made their way to the front of Andrea's house and sat on the sidewalk watching the humans look around. When they seemed to be coming close to Hector's tunnel, Frederick motioned toward the little dog.

"Bark as loud and as much as you can."

Hector was only too happy to comply as he barked from the top of his lungs. Several humans looked in their direction and called Andrea and Alice.

"Hector!" the woman exclaimed when she saw him.

"Oh, you naughty boy, how did you get out?" Andrea kissed him and took the dog inside.

Alice stared at Frederick who now curled himself up on the porch rug under the chair swing.

"Why do I think you are the cause of Hector's escape?" she muttered under her breath. "I think you need to be in your kennel, mister."

A. Nation

Scooping him up into her arms, she carried the large cat inside through the front door.

The cat and dog were sleeping in the kitchen when they noticed Alice and Andrea talking. Hector and Frederick got up and strolled in believing there must be food if humans are at the table. Hector stood up on his stubby back legs pawing at Andrea's slacks.

"No, you get down. Mummy will feed you later."

Frederick watched; and when Hector got nothing, the cat sauntered into the living room hopping on top of one of the chairs by the picture window to look outside.

One day Hector and Frederick snuck out again from Andrea's yard into the neighbor's again, but this time the owner spotted them.

"Shoo, go back home," he stood waving his arms.

"Come, Heck, there is someone visiting our humans."

"It's Mary. Race ya," the short legged dog barked.

The two animals scurried through the open fence gate. Frederick saw a car door open.

This new person to Frederick walked around her car and shut the door without noticing the animals laying low in the back floorboard.

Hector started to whine. *"What are we going to do?"*

"Sit tight, she'll be back."

"I don't like riding in this box. Every time I do, I end up at the groomer or the vet."

A. Nation

"This is a different human, let's see what happens."

Mary came back after five minutes. She was planning to stop at the Post Office, the police station, and then Lost Keepsakes to see how her new cousin was doing.

Hector perked up but Frederick pushed the dog's head back down to the floorboard with his paw. *"Be quiet,"* the big cat hissed when Mary engaged the noisy controls.

She stopped and talked to a man.

"What is it, officer?" they heard her say.

"We have a delicate situation inside the antique shop and ask that you turn around and go home," said the young man.

"I just got my badge today. Can I join you?"

"All right, pull over to the far end of the street. We're over on your right."

Mary drove her car down to the end of the road where the young officer indicated and opened her door.

"Now!" Frederick hissed. Scaring Mary as the two animals bolted through the center and out her front door, they soon ran into one of the hedges.

In the back of the building, the kitchen door had been opened for ventilation. Frederick and Hector entered the antique shop and headed to the bedroom display. Frederick ran to the main area of the shop, leaped up onto one of the built in wall shelves, and peered down to see Hector climb onto one of the single beds in the exhibit.

"Yip!"

"Quiet, do you want them to find us?"

A. Nation

"No."

A large man began running out into the main room of the shop and frightened Frederick and Hector. The little dog scurried under one of the beds. Frederick jumped down from a shelf with claws extended landing on top of the big man's head and shoulders.

"Aheee, get this off me, help!" he cried out in pain.

The burly man ran out the front door with Frederick still clinging to his jacket. The cat bit his left ear and jumped down when he saw the humans waiting to grab the unwanted guest.

Hector poked his head out of the front door and stood near Frederick. He gained more appreciation for this brave cat and decided to start barking.

Humans and animals watched as the man and his buddies were shoved into the patrol cars and taken back to the city station. Mary came up behind both animals and scooped them up into each arm.

"What will become of you two if you keep escaping," she chided them.

After she checked out with the duty officer, she drove back to Andrea's home. Parking her vehicle, she opened the door to see one set of sorrowful eyes. Frederick just stared. Once again she picked them up into each arm and headed for the front door. As her arms were full, she was glad that the automatic doorbell registered her, ringing throughout the house.

Alice answered the door.

A. Nation

"Mary, you found them," she exclaimed taking Frederick from her. Mary could hear Andrea crying as loud as possible.

"Andrea, Mary found Hector."

Alice looked down at Frederick. The cat ignored her and walked off into the kitchen to see if any food had been poured.

A. Nation

The Farm

The time had come for Alice and Mike to leave Montrose. Alice laid her folded clothes into her suitcase on her bed. "I can't either, but I'm glad I could come and help you." Frederick hopped up and stepped into Alice's case.

"Oh no, you don't," she said picking her cat up. Guiding him into his kennel cage, he let out a resounding "Yeow."

She picked him up and pushed him into his kennel. Frederick was scratching the door of his cage while Hector sniffed at him.

"Where are you going, Fred? How come you are in there?" the dachshund asked.

"They're taking me some place again," He growled.

"Will you come back?"

"Don't know. Bye Hector."

Alice picked up the cat cage as they all proceeded out to their waiting car. James, Andrea's husband, helped carry one of their bags and helped Mike place them in the cargo holder. Frederick was placed on one of the seats inside.

Alice and Mike made the trip to Denver in a little over four and a half hours stopping for lunch and cat exercise. When they checked into their hotel they had to pay extra to keep Frederick in the room. After washing up, Frederick heard Mike's device ring.

A. Nation

"Yeah, we can be there. Bye."

"The major wants to see us," he said.

Once again Frederick was regulated to his kennel.

Later, after the humans had left him alone, they returned.

When Alice walked into their motel room, she stopped and opened the cage. Frederick bounded out. She gathered the large feline into her arms and sat on a nearby chair.

"Oh, Freddy you liked Ralph didn't you? Sure you did. You remember the Reverend here? He's going to take you back to Arizona." She gave him a gentle hug and put him back into his kennel. "I'm going to use the bathroom, Reverend. Why don't you take Frederick now? Have a safe trip." With that, she entered the small bathroom and closed the door after her.

"I guess that's your cue," Mike said shaking his hand and handing over the cage.

"I'll let you know when I arrive. Goodbye all," Reverend Phillips said.

Frederick remembered this human was called Reverend from his stay on Mars. *"Where's Alice?"* he asked himself. The man loaded him and his kennel onto a shuttle. The next thing he knew, after a few hours, he was back on the farm in Arizona.

Jan fed him and he found a nice soft spot on one of the beds. One of his eyes opened when he heard his name mentioned as she talked.

A. Nation

"Everything is just fine. As soon as the reverend arrived, Fredrick found a comfortable spot on my bed."

Frederick was sleeping on the new people's bed when a beeping woke him up. He raised one eye and then the other when the human, called Alex, struggled to answer the noisy device. Frederick had a nice warm spot at the end of their bed and didn't want to move.

"Don't answer," he heard the woman, Jan, whisper.

"Uggghhh, I have to," the man sighed.

Frederick saw her face appeared at the edge of the man's brown shoulders as she smoothed away his long black hair.

"For all they know, you're in the shower," she cooed.

"You're an evil woman," he smirked.

"It comes with the territory."

His long muscular arm reached for his comphone and received only a handful of hair from Frederick, who yowled as he jumped off the bed. Alex grabbed the device on the fourth ring.

"Yeah, what's up?" he muttered into the comphone. "Can't get anyone else?" He felt a soft punch to his backside. "Yeah, okay, be there this afternoon."

Turning toward Jan, "I have to go, business, sorry."

"Alex, you owe me," she said rolling away from him.

"And I will gladly repay in interest."

"Right and I'm just a peanut butter and jelly sandwich," she teased.

A. Nation

"I'd like that too," he said grinning at her.

Frederick left the bedroom after the rude disturbance and curled up in his favorite spot on the sofa. Falling into another snooze, he perked up one ear to the dog howling outside.

His humans were up and Jan began to make breakfast.

"Yeah, breakfast about ready?" the man said, sitting down at the kitchen table.

"First, you need to feed Ralph and check on Carmelia before you go," she replied.

"A man's work is never done," he said, rising out of his chair.

Frederick watched the man his mistress called Alex walk out the front door. He could see Ralph standing and panting from his announcements.

After a time, the front door opened and the tall man returned. Frederick sat staring at him in the middle of the bare wood floor upon one of the scattered throw rugs. He wanted his breakfast too.

"Yeow," he growled.

"It's coming, just be patient," his mistress replied, peeling off the can lid of cat food. When his ears twitched toward the sound of tearing of steel, he padded over to the edge of her long skirt. He raised his head to watch as she scooped the moist bits into his food bowl on the counter by the sink.

"Here you go Freddy," Jan announced, taking his full bowl to the mat near corner wall. Like a magnet, the cat's

A. Nation

face followed his food bowl until it was set down on the floor.

While he ate, Alex commented, "How come these animals get fed before I do?"

"Because I don't want them in my way when we eat," Jan replied.

Ralph made a lot of noise barking. Frederick, just finishing his morsels of food, watched as another man entered the dwelling. Then he heard Jan mention his name.

"Come on Frederick. You need to go outside," she said, picking him up into her arms.

Passing the shaggy dog's head, Frederick looked down as Jan carried him toward the front yard.

Ralph perked up. Even though the dog was used to the cat, sometimes his basic instinct kicked into gear whenever he saw Frederick.

"Hey cat, where are you goin'?"

"None of your beeswax dog."

"My name is Ralph," he barked.

"Whatever."

Jan put Frederick down onto the dusty soil about ten feet away from the dog's restraint. That way the cat had a choice of whether or not to move closer without triggering the dog's chasing desire.

"Both of you behave. Go, Freddy, do your business," Jan told them and walked toward the barn.

A. Nation

"There's more goats out there," Ralph whined.

"What do you mean more goats?"

"I heard the humans last night and then there were three."

"That's not fair." Frederick did his business by the barn corner wall and peeked in.

He sniffed the odd odor of another animal and poked his head through the crack in the barn door. His mistress retrieved the hose to fill up the water container hanging on the fence line. Jan opened the stall door next to the goats and began sweeping out the old stained and manured straw stalks from the night before. She reached toward a nearby fresh bale of straw. She opened Carmelia's pen and led the nanny goat by the horn from her stall which forced the kids to follow into their clean pen.

Jan then closed the slatted fencing across the stall and left the barn. The nanny goat sniffed around and could sense another presence in the barn.

"Baaaa. Alert! Cat about. Hide youngins"

"Ralph told me you have kits," Frederick mewed.

"Kids, you fanged beast. Did you say, Ralph? I never trust a wolf. Baaaaa."

Frederick, not wanting a stab from the goat's horns, backed out from the doorway and headed toward the front steps. Ralph was still panting from the excitement of the visitor and the warm autumn air.

"Well?" Ralph woofed.

A. Nation

"Yes, you were right, but she doesn't like me much. She thinks you're a wolf."

"Awwwwwooooooo. Maybe I am," he howled as much as a dog can smirk while he lay down on the wooden floorboards of the porch. Frederick followed suit and curled up nearby in the morning sun.

After a long nap, Frederick stretched and jumped down to the floor. He strolled over to the open front doorway and sat on the threshold flicking his tail.

"He left," Ralph moaned.

"Who?"

"My master. Fred, don't you care about anything?"

"This is my caring face," he said not moving a facial muscle.

Ralph stared and couldn't see a difference. Then Frederick continued on.

"Is my food bowl filled?—Yes.

"Is my water bowl full?—Yes.

"Do I have a warm dry bed?—Yes. Well, then I guess I do care about something."

"It's not always about you, cat," he ruffed.

"You and humans have to be so complicated. Of course, it's all about me." Done with the conversation, Frederick turned his back and sauntered back toward Jan's bedroom. There he hopped onto the bed to find a comfortable spot against the Navajo decorated pillows Jan

A. Nation

had purchased at last year's fair. Within minutes, he was asleep.

The next morning his new mistress awoke and rose around seven o'clock and flopped her small suitcase on the foot of the bed. Frederick, who was still snoozing, opened one eye and then the other. Noticing his mistress was putting things into the container, his memory clicked with anticipation. In the recesses of his memory, a flash of Alice's face reminded him that this human was following the same routine.

Jan turned her back to retrieve a small box that contained a silver necklace with a dark blue topaz set in a teardrop setting. When she proceeded to place the packet into her suitcase, there was Frederick staring at her in the center of her folded clothes.

"Whoa fella," Jan coaxed while picking him up with care as to not cause his claws to extend on her nice blue blouse. "You, my friend, are staying here," she whispered as she placed the cat down on the floor.

"I'll only be gone a day and Naomi will take care of all of you," she added as if the cat understood.

Frederick looked up at the human who just said, "blah, blah, blah." Without the word 'treats' mentioned he headed toward the open doorway.

He could see Ralph sleeping on the porch.
"Ralph, wake up," he meowed.
"Ruff, hmm, what?"
"The human is leaving."

A. Nation

"No. What? How do you know?"

"She's putting her skins into a box. I've seen this done before and this time, she's not taking me."

Ralph chose to not notice Frederick being self-centered again and whined.

"No, I don't want her to go. Mom did this before and stayed away a long time." He began to howl which began a ruckus in the barn.

Jan stepped out on the porch when she heard the howling.

"What in the world has got into you, boy? Hush up, you're scaring the goats."

Ralph began to jump toward her, but Jan moved away in time. Frederick just stared at the dog's antics.

Just then they could see dust stirring up on the horizon down the road. The car stopped in front of the steps and both dene' women exited the vehicle. Jan walked down to greet them. One was carrying a small case.

Walking back up the three steps to the porch, Jan reached for Ralph's collar, restraining him, to allow her guests pass inside.

Frederick turned his ears to the new voices. He only picked up a few words about Ralph, some dogs, and the goat."

"Yes, Frederick is over there on the couch. He can come and go as he pleases and will come back as long as his bowls are filled."

"I'll watch them. Don't you worry."

A. Nation

"Are you ready to go?" the other woman asked.

"Yup. Oh, Frederick usually stays and sleeps inside. They both get along but Ralph can be impulsive."

"Don't you worry. Go on. They'll be fine. I have Sunflower's number, what's yours?"

Jan relayed her comphone number. "Perfect, well, let's go," she said and followed Sunflower out to the car.

Frederick gazed at Ralph as he began straining on his rope when his mistress and the other woman entered the vehicle. That is when he realized a strange human was standing in the doorway.

"Ruff," he said establishing his territory.

"You behave yourself and we'll get along fine," Naomi said shutting the front door in his face.

Frederick turned and ran into Jan's bedroom to hop on top of the bed.

Many days later, after his mistress had returned, she entered the bed room closet and began grabbing several clothes. Frederick sat on her bed watching this whole process. Attempting to climb into one of Jan's suitcases, he was shooed away by her wild hand gestures. Ralph was barking up a storm when Jan snapped the bags closed and walked by Frederick, without a glance. He jumped down from the bed and followed her to the doorway. The woman who came before when his mistress left was standing on the porch. Bored, he wandered over to the couch and jumped into his favorite spot.

A. Nation

Frederick was snoozing on the end of the couch when the men entered. He popped his head up and jumped down to the floor. Giving them a hesitated stare, he scurried into Jan's bedroom.

A. Nation

Commotion

Days passed into weeks. Frederick slept and ate his days away. Jan was home when two men stopped by. Frederick knew the Frank man but not the other. Ralph was barking his usual when the men entered the home dragging the huge mix breed into the spare room where Frederick was taking a snooze on the bed. His ears twitched when the sound of bleating goats arouse his curiosity. Meanwhile, Ralph was licking the window.

Frederick sat on the spare bed watching the dog pace back and forth from the door to the glass.

"Will you settle down? I can't get my sleep," the cat complained.

"Got to get outside. Bad guys again. Could hurt my mom," he whined.

"Let the humans do their thing. It's none of my affair."

"Humans feed you too. You should care," Ralph barked.

Frederick brought his head up, *"If you don't be quiet, the bad ones will get you too."*

Ralph stopped for a minute to allow that thought to settle in his small brain. Then he began to growl and whimper at the same time.

"Yeow," Frederick moaned placing his paws over his black ears.

A. Nation

Ralph kept running at the window, bumping the glass with his head until the pane shattered. Frederick watched how the animal jumped through the broken glass to the outside. The sound of Ralph's high pitched barking continued for a few minutes until a sharp explosion cracked through the air.

Frederick sat up on the corner end of the bed when he heard Ralph's bark again. A woman, who had stayed before in this house, opened the door. Frederick jumped down and ran passed her legs.

~Fatal Error Death by Innocence~

Several months had passed since that day when his mistress made a funny sound at the breakfast table.

"Aaggkk," Jan moaned in frustration.

From the couch, the black and white cat, Frederick, lifted his head from his sofa position to see where the strange sound Jan had made came from. He watched them leave when a noisy vehicle pulled up in front of their porch. Ralph as usual was barking.

Frederick slept until Jan entered the home. Alex wasn't present. He yawned and stretched. Jumping down from the couch, he checked his food bowl. Finding it empty, he drank some water.

Then all of a sudden, his mistress yelled.

"Carmelia, Carmelia," she called and ran out the front door.

He followed her out and stood in the open doorway.

The dog, who had seen the goat, jerked his head up.

A. Nation

"Wha–Where's the goat? What's going on?" he said, shaking his head looking for something to bark at.

"What are you talking about?" Frederick asked him.

"The goat was in the yard and my mistress ran after it."

"So?"

"I'll never understand you, Fred," Ralph huffed and sat down.

"I think I'll find a good spot on that couch," Frederick said, returning into the house.

"Don't you want to know more about the goat?" Ralph barked as the cat entered the home.

Frederick turned around. "Do I look like I care?"

He turned again and hopped onto the soft sofa.

The next day Alex loaded Frederick in his kennel and by 1:00 pm, they had arrived at Alex's apartment in Tucson. There they unloaded their luggage and Frederick into the small two-bedroom apartment he rented.

When Frederick was let out, he darted into the nearest room to hide out. He sniffed around and could detect Alex's scent when Jan entered the bedroom.

"I'm going shopping. I put your food and water out and here is your tray," she said, pointing at the metal container in the bathroom.

"Yeow."

"Now, you be good. I just have to leave for now," she said, closing the door in his face.

A. Nation

He strolled over to the couch in the center of the room and found a soft area to curl up in.

Later she returned with some large crinkling tote bags. Alex came home and noticed the shopping parcels leaning near the bedroom wall. Frederick was pawing one of the clothing totes when Jan admonished him.

"Freddy, you stay out of there. I already stored your food."

The cat looked up in surprise and ran to the sofa. With one great leap, he bounded up onto one of the light blue cushions.

Alex eased himself down into one of the straight back chairs near the kitchen table.

After they ate dinner, Jan cleaned up the table and put the dirty dishes into the dishwasher. Alex moved over to the sofa and brushed Frederick off with the back of his hand to make room for Jan when she finished. The cat chose the nearby upholstered chair and jumped onto the cushion. The humans began talking in soft voices lulling him to sleep.

When they stood up and walked into their bedroom, Frederick jumped back on the couch where Alex warmed a spot to settle in for the night. The scrolling on the video machine was becoming an irritation until he slapped the remote off the cushion onto the floor. As if by design, the controller turned to the animal channel. Frederick was mesmerized until he fell asleep just as the screen displayed a lion and his mate.

A. Nation

In the dark of night, Frederick jumped off the bed and ran into the living area of the house. He was awake. He wanted to play. First he ran around the sofa and hopped up to the sink and counter. He saw a long metal object and pushed it off. The clang from hitting the floor caused the humans to mutter something. He jumped down and noting his food bowl was empty, he pranced over to the bedroom door.

Alex came to the doorway, wrapping the ties around his robe. Frederick just stood on the floor before him in the main room staring up at him

"I'll let Jan feed you. I don't want you going hungry on our flight," he whispered, walking past the cat and opening up the fridge.

"Meow," he replied, smelling the aroma of food items.

After Alex fixed something, he placed the food back into the cooler. He returned to the bedroom to dress and returned with a small tote. He opened the fridge again and ate one of the sandwiches he had made, washing the quick meal down with a glass of orange juice. He packed the other wrapped meal into the small cooler to put into his car. He checked on Jan again and made it out the door before Frederick could escape.

Three days later, Frederick was packed up again and placed inside into the moving vehicle. The humans parked their car and carried him into a noisy building that reminded him of his former mistress. He was loaded onto a dolly cart with the rest of the luggage.

There seemed to be a lot of talking until Jan sat down and remembered the cat crate they had been towing around. "I'd better feed, Frederick."

After he finished his meal, Jan sat down in the waiting area and placed Frederick's kennel on the floor. A lady set her luggage and another kennel down opposite the cat.

Frederick became alert when he saw what was scratching in the other kennel cage.

A small dog with nose whiskers and pointed ears stared back at him. The dog began yapping until the woman tapped on the top of the cage.

"Hush up, Tommy, they won't let us on if you're making a racket. Sorry, but he's just nervous and I see you have a cat," the woman said.

"Yes, this cat has already been to Mars and the Moon," Jan relayed.

While the humans talked, Frederick spoke his mind to the little dog.

"What are you yapping about, brownie?" Frederick remarked, referencing the dog's coloring.

"Cat, cat? My name is Tommy, thank you very much."

"Well, keep it down or the humans will throw you away and you'll never see your human again," Frederick said, curling his lips at the canine.

The dog began whining.

A. Nation

"What's the matter, sweetie, everything is going to be all right. Just lie down and go to sleep," said the woman.

"Where are you going?" Frederick asked.

"Nuu York, I think. That's what it sounded like and you?"

"I'm going to Mars."

"Where's Mars?"

"I don't know. But I do know it takes a long time to get there," Frederick replied.

"Well, Freddy, it's about time that I take you to the restroom," Jan said to her cat.

Jan rose out of her seat and pulled the kennel on wheels through the sparse crowd of people.

Later, two women stopped near his kennel. The younger one discovered Frederick.

"Yeow"

"Oh, you brought a kitty," Tiffany exclaimed and dropped to the floor to look at Frederick through the cage opening.

"Why couldn't we take Hector?" Tiffany asked, thinking about their little dachshund they left home.

Andrea ignored the question and smiled when she saw Alex's wife, Jan.

Jan looked up, "Andrea. Good to see you again. It will be nice to travel with a face I recognize."

"Can I take the cat out?" Tiffany asked, poking her finger through the kennel gate. Frederick placed his paw on her finger.

A. Nation

"No, he would run away. He's been to Mars before. Did you know that?" Jan asked.

Frederick felt himself lifted into the air by Alex. He and Jan headed toward their ship. They walked a ways to the landing and up a couple of steps into the fuselage of the immense transport. He was carried, set down, picked up, and set down again until Frederick made his presence known.

"Yeow" Frederick howled.

"We're almost to our room, Freddy. I haven't forgotten you," Jan said as they arrived at their cabin door. Once Alex had shut the door, Jan undid the cat litter tray beneath the kennel.

Once she wrapped the waste up and deposited it into the refuse can for incineration later, Alex let the black and white cat out of his prison. He had to move fast as the feline didn't have his gravity weights on his body or legs.

She cleaned his litter tray and let him run around until she returned the repapered tray back under his carrier. She scooped him up and put him back inside the kennel.

"I'm sorry, Fred, but Alice was very clear to me how you might escape. I'll let you run around tonight, okay?"

"Yeow," Frederick replied only understanding that he wasn't going keep his freedom in the room.

A. Nation

Red Planet

After Frederick's routine was stable, he noticed his mistress filling her suitcase with clothes again. Strange men dropped off larger pieces of luggage for the humans to fill. He tried a third time to step into the container when Alex picked him up and set him inside his kennel.

"Well, I don't see where we left anything," Jan said looking around their small cabin one more time and in the toilet area for the third time.

"I got Frederick," Alex said holding the cat carrier.

"Here, I'll take him and you can pull the bags," said Jan lifting up the carrier.

He watched through the gate grill at all the human legs moving by his cage until Alex lifted him up and set him and his carrier on the floor near Jan. She started to walk up another ramp but found a chair nearby where she and Frederick could wait. She could see the entire concourse from her position.

The ride in the smaller craft was smooth until the shuttle descended toward the Mars Space Station located in Galle Crater. Jan and the other woman continued talking until the shuttle glided into a landing position. Frederick didn't like the absence of gravity as he tried to find a comfortable spot in the carrier.

A. Nation

"Yeow," he protested, feeling hungry, but received no attention.

The shuttle shook and came to an abrupt stop. Alex reached down and picked up the cat kennel. Frederick could see his mistress in front.

Once they found their compartment on the space station. Jan pulled out his food dish and opened a can of his food.

Then one day while he was cleaning his paws in his kennel, Jan came through cabin door and a familiar human entered behind her. Frederick stared from behind the kennel's barred gate. The woman came closer and the smell was someone he knew.

"Oh, Freddy," Alice said as Jan closed the door behind them.

Jan reached over to the carrier to open the small door.

Frederick stuck his head out and then one paw and another.

"Hi, Frederick, do you remember me?" Alice asked.

The cat crept closer and waved a paw at her face.

"Meow"

He jumped down from the bed where the carrier sat and circled his former mistress's feet. Jan pulled open a drawer and gave Alice the small bag of treats.

Alice sat down on the bed and offered him a treat from the small bag. Frederick sniffed the morsel and took a bite.

A. Nation

"I guess I have to ask you now that Frederick is here, do you want him to stay?" Jan asked.

"Honestly, I'll have to think about that. I have Nathan to take care of for now."

"Maybe Nathan would like a pet?"

"He would."

"How about I bring Frederick to your cabin after your son gets out of daycare. Then you can decide from there."

"That's evil, Jan, but that would better than at the daycare where I can't control the other children wanting to pet a cat. Okay, we'll see."

He ate the chicken treats and rubbed up against Alice's leg.

"See, he does remember you," Jan said.

The women continued talking until Jan placed him into the kennel.

A few days later, he found himself in Alice's cabin with a short and immature human who wanted to pet him all the time.

Frederick stayed on Mars with the Carone family, not caring one way or another as long as he was fed and kept warm. One of the tall beings from another town brought over one of the cloned cats created a few years ago which doubled the mischief they were able to get into. A couple of years had passed when Alice relinquished her hold on him to another friend returning to Earth. Jan took him back to live out his days on the farm.

Epilogue

Frederick will never die not only because his story is fiction and will relive over and over by the reading of my books.

Cherish every moment you have with your pets because the real ones die too soon.

About the Author

I realized after the eighth book that I had written, there were many adventures about an interesting cat I had wrote about. So, I compiled all those entries into one novelette. Most of this is in the cat's POV with some dialog from the humans to give you a sense where the scenes take place in the series.

I hoped you enjoyed this story and if you want to know the full story of the adventures of Frederick the cat, begin with the first book called, *Similar But Not the Same*.

A. Nation travels the west with her husband. This is her first novelette.

For more insights and new releases to how my stories progressed, see my blog at:

bloggingwrites.weebly.com and

books2read.com/author/a-nation/subscribe/1/28898/

You can also find information on my books at:

Facebook under **A. Nation Books** and **A. Nation Author.**

A. Nation

A. Nation

Coupon on Next Page

A. Nation

Book coupon
Return for
$1.00 Off Price
On 1 eBook, paperback, or pack
anation347@yahoo.com
No Expiration unless I do
Present this coupon in person

Made in the USA
Columbia, SC
27 December 2019